T0134792

THE STAINED
Tablecloth

ANGELA BEAUMAN

Copyright © 2020 Angela Beauman.

All rights reserved. No part of this book may be used or reproduced by any means, graphic, electronic, or mechanical, including photocopying, recording, taping or by any information storage retrieval system without the written permission of the author except in the case of brief quotations embodied in critical articles and reviews.

This is a work of fiction. All of the characters, names, incidents, organizations, and dialogue in this novel are either the products of the author's imagination or are used fictitiously.

WestBow Press books may be ordered through booksellers or by contacting:

WestBow Press
A Division of Thomas Nelson & Zondervan
1663 Liberty Drive
Bloomington, IN 47403
www.westbowpress.com
1 (866) 928-1240

Because of the dynamic nature of the Internet, any web addresses or links contained in this book may have changed since publication and may no longer be valid. The views expressed in this work are solely those of the author and do not necessarily reflect the views of the publisher, and the publisher hereby disclaims any responsibility for them.

Any people depicted in stock imagery provided by Getty Images are models, and such images are being used for illustrative purposes only.
Certain stock imagery © Getty Images.

Scripture quotations taken from the New American Standard Bible® (NASB),
Copyright © 1960, 1962, 1963, 1968, 1971, 1972, 1973,
1975, 1977, 1995 by The Lockman Foundation
Used by permission. www.Lockman.org

ISBN: 978-1-9736-8784-9 (sc)
ISBN: 978-1-9736-8785-6 (e)

Library of Congress Control Number: 2020904618

Print information available on the last page.

WestBow Press rev. date: 03/18/2020

WESTBOW
PRESS®
A DIVISION OF THOMAS NELSON
& ZONDERVAN

An old man from church was cleaning out his small apartment, which was filled with a lifetime of memories. Five pianos from his pianist days, old computers and office equipment from his days as an insurance salesman, and old pots, pans, silverware, and serving platters from days when he had family around... when. Perhaps he was a bit of a hoarder?

Each week, after church he would say, "come to the car I have more stuff for you".

One Sunday, he gave me a tablecloth. Warning me that it was stained, I reluctantly took the tablecloth, thanked him, and drove away.

It was a faded white tablecloth, with flowers embroidered throughout, Italian lace trimmed the entire perimeter, and yes indeed, it was stained. Whether or not I would use it, I knew the old man thought highly enough of me that I should have it. He said that it was handmade in Italy and it belonged to his mother. As he was in his mid-eighties, it was obvious that his mother had passed away many years ago. Indeed, it was what you might call outdated, but it was also so charmingly nostalgic. I thought, "I wonder how many times this was used to celebrate birthdays or Christmas"?

I wondered if it was around when someone got some bad news? Maybe it was used during a last meal to send off a loved one they would never see again. I wondered what stories the stained tablecloth would tell if it could speak. I also wondered about each stain, and who made it. Maybe stains were made by small children learning to maneuver their tiny hands, maybe by older people trying I control their aging hands. When the old man gave me the stained tablecloth, were memories of good times or bad running through his head? Was it used to catch tears of laughter or tears of sorrow?

I gently placed it in the washer and added some soap. Some time later, I went back and checked to see how clean I was able to get it. The stains remained. They wouldn't budge. I hung it out to dry, trying to avoid having to iron it. Once dry, I examined the stains carefully. Like a detective examining a crime scene, I scrutinized each stain. Looking at the color, size, and shape of each stain. I tried to figure out what food or drink may have made the stain, and how long it had been there. I put the tablecloth right up to one eye, and tightly closed the other as if I could control the focus like a microscope if I closed it tight enough.

Wanting to see if I could capture the entire story all at once, I threw it open over my kitchen table as if opening a parachute. In what seemed like slow motion, I watched as the stained tablecloth gently floated above the table then landed as delicately as a feather tossed in the wind finding its place to settle. Starting at one corner, I lifted it up section by section.

I was like a detective in old noir movies questioning a suspect. The sun was like my partner assisting me by shining like a spotlight directly in the face of each stain, asking it to reveal itself- give up its alibi. As the wind moved the leaves on the trees outside, it's light danced around on the tablecloth again, like a swinging light above a suspect. In the center were two relatively round, dark gray stains- almost burns actually, perhaps where candles had burned too low in a subpar holder.

I could almost surmise how many people could gather around at any given time. Perhaps it was set for six people, maybe eight. Maybe there were days when people gathered around so tightly, there wasn't any room for comfort at all, just the comfort of being together. Maybe there were days when someone dined alone. My detective brain identified that stains were made where plates would be set for people to gather and dine together.

Stains were discovered on either head end of the table, with additional stains on each longer side, where two or three sat side by side. Many stains were found down the center of the tablecloth, running end to end. I'd imagine as the food was placed near the center of the table, running lengthwise, stains would be made as people would fill their plates and maybe spill something delicious before the plates were able to catch the food. Maybe there was a joke made right before the exchange took place, or maybe a word which angered someone, causing hands to shake and food to be dropped.

Were the red stains from glasses of wine
used to celebrate something?

Maybe the red stains were from meatballs falling off
of a too-small spoon on their way to a plate.

Could the rainbow of colors found near a head end of the tablecloth be from the colorful icing on a birthday cake? Regardless of what I attempted to speculate, the tablecloth was still stained-perhaps permanently.

My mind started to wander... wanting to know more, wanting to hear the stories, wanting to see the faces, wanting to hear the voices, wanting to wipe the tears.

Suddenly, it didn't matter to me that the tablecloth was stained, because it was a relic of life celebrated, and people to celebrate with. In its history was laughter, and sorrow, abundance, or maybe want. The old man was the only one who could tell the story of its past. I wanted to know. Blessed with a big family, we always had many people gather around our table.

The old man was now alone most of the time. Sure, there was a friend or two and distant relatives too far away for regular visits. At his age, it was harder to gather the people. Driving was difficult and schedules were full. All he had to rely on were fading memories.

Maybe it was time to make new stains. The following Sunday, I saw the old man again. Greeting him with a kiss on the cheek, we exchanged pleasantries, and I invited him to join my family for dinner. He excitedly accepted!

Hours later, he was at our home like an impatient child on Christmas morning anxious to open the colorfully wrapped presents. He walked in, and immediately noticed his tablecloth. In an instant all was revealed to me, all my questions were answered. The tablecloth spoke through the look on the old man's face, and in his eyes.

We sat, prayed, and dinner was served.

There was robust laughter, pleasant conversation, a few tears, and lots of new stains. Although he was present with us, I knew he was reliving a time when the tablecloth was in his possession, and his family was with him. I was all too happy to be a part of new memories, and new stains in the latter years of his life.

We continue to share meals together- my family and the old man, and we listen to his stories and watch his eyes grow younger as he grows older.

You see, it wasn't about an old man cleaning out his house and giving things away, It was about having someone to share stories and laughter with. It was about loving one another. It was about friendship and family. It was about spending time together. It was about making an old man feel wanted. It was about making a stranger... family.

We will have the tablecloth for many years, until it is time to pass it down to my children... Making stains one day at a time.

So next time you unfurl your tablecloth, make sure you relish all the stains of happiness, laughter, and love.

John 15:12 "This is my commandment, that you love one another as I have loved you".

Author Biography

Angela Beauman is a native Long Islander, and has been married to her handsome, green-eyed husband for 26 years. She has two wonderful children, and graduated summa cum laude from "The Culinary Academy of my Momma". She's also a professional cookie maker, Zumba fanatic, driver's seat singer, and makes friends on a grocery store check out line.

Printed in the United States
By Bookmasters